FAR in the DAY

FAR in the DAY

BY JULIA CUNNINGHAM

Illustrated by

DON FREEMAN

A YEARLING BOOK

Published by
Dell Publishing Co., Inc.
1 Dag Hammarskjold Plaza
New York, New York 10017

Yearling ® TM 913705, Dell Publishing Co., Inc.

ISBN: 0-440-43185-9

Reprinted by arrangement with Pantheon Books,
a division of Random House, Inc.

Printed in the United States of America
First Yearling printing—November 1980

CW

FOR CLYDE ROBERT BULLA

ARTIST OF A GREATER CIRCUS

WITH LOVE

FAR in the DAY

1

The curtain of steam from the stewpot parted and there, in front of the long, green line of land, stood a boy.

"The saints preserve us!" cried out one of the five seated at the trestle-table that was set in the center of a clearing bounded by three trailers and a large tent.

"Nothing to fear, Jimsey," said the tall, dark man at the head. "He's not a ghost. See, he's solid in his clothes. Most likely a tinker's son."

"Michael," said the one woman, "I saw him before—yesterday afternoon as we stopped for the night. With as filthy a group as ever stole for a living." The bright purple dress strained over her bulges as she leaned forward.

"No need to judge the boy before he's had a chance to speak," said Michael Duffy.

They waited, each in his own way: the fat woman so tensely that the flesh overlapping her collarbones quivered; Jimsey, his features caught in a nervous twist; a pale boy of nine half-smiling as though in welcome; a large, musclebound man vacantly, his attention on the rich odors from the stew; and lastly, Michael Duffy—his lean face allowing only severity—the owner of the faded blue circus tent that billowed emptily with each stir of air.

But there was no reply from the narrow stillness of the figure in front of them. Even his body seemed to intensify the quiet. He also waited.

"Must be an idiot," grunted Madame Creel, her eyes, pouched about by fat, somehow satisfied, as though they were feeding on the helplessness of the stranger.

"What's your name?" asked the child.

No answer, only an unfolding of his hands at his sides.

"He doesn't know," interpreted Jimsey. He got up from the table and approached the boy. "We're friends," he began slowly. "We won't hurt you. Tell us where you came from." No response quickened the boy's face. Only his eyes spoke for him as they stared into Jimsey's, bewildered and uncomprehending. "You hungry?" The circus clown's stubby hand gestured toward the open pot of stew.

The boy hesitated and then nodded.

"Dirty little beggar," exclaimed Madame Creel. "Just what I suspected. He's here to cage a meal." She turned to Michael Duffy. "Chase him off."

A heaviness seemed to fall upon the man's shoulders,

bowing them. He looked to Phillip, so solid he seemed staked into the ground. "Serve up what we have with a bowl for the boy. He can eat and go." And a few minutes later as the circus owner forked up the few floating chunks of carrots and potatoes from the hot and greasy gravy, he retreated entirely from the group around him and no longer listened.

"Move down a little, Billy," said Jimsey to the child. "Make room for our guest."

The fat woman guffawed. "Guest, is he? Royalty maybe? You're as much an idiot as he is, Jimsey! A third-rate clown in an Irish circus so run down we've got no animals but a horse as old as my fortune cards and a toothless bear!" Her bitterness did not penetrate the abstraction of Duffy. The clown turned his back on her but the muscles in his left cheek jerked in spasm.

"I'm Billy Bill," the child said to the stranger as he slipped swiftly into the space on the bench. "I am the bareback rider of the Michael Duffy Circus. I even have my own costume."

The silent boy ate quickly, offering Billy a smile so small it was not visible to anyone else.

Billy laughed. "I knew you'd like us. As soon as supper is over I'll introduce you to Sir William. He's our bear."

"You'll do nothing of the sort!" Madame Creel's jowls had reddened. "Out he goes right now! Just what this business needs, another stomach to fill, especially one that belongs to a deaf and dumb tinker's bastard."

The clown's mouth relaxed and he looked directly into the woman's anger. "Billy's mother never allowed bad language in front of the boy."

"A pity!" was Madame Creel's reaction. "Might have toughened him up a bit. Miranda too, weak thing that she was."

Michael Duffy rose up into his tallness. "Miranda's name is never to be mentioned. I thought that had been understood." But he was halfway to his trailer by the time Madame Creel huffed out a reluctant "Sorry, I forgot" and did not hear it.

The little boy patted the older one's arm. "Don't be afraid. You don't have to go into the dark. You can sleep with me."

"That he cannot!" said the fat woman.

"Then with Sir William," said Billy. "He's sort of like Sir William. He can't talk either. But I like him. The only thing is, I don't know what to call him."

Jimsey stopped stacking the plates for a moment and gazed into the indigo of the evening. "I know, Billy," he said at last. "Remember that road you wanted to explore yesterday only we didn't have enough time?"

"Oh, yes! It was walled all the way down."

"Did you read the name of it?"

The boy ran to the clown and hugged him hard. "Tallow! That's it, Jimsey!" He ran back to the stranger, reached up, and touched him on the right shoulder. "I hereby dub you Sir Tallow, Tallow for short."

"That's enough nonsense for one night!" grunted Madame Creel. "Jimsey, get to the wash-up and you, Billy, to bed. Phillip can sit by me while I read the cards." Their obedience was instant. Only Tallow was left without direction. For a little while he stood behind the great lump of a woman and watched her deal out a cross-pattern of upturned cards. If anyone had been there to observe him he would have seen the look of listening and in his frown the effort to understand.

"It's no good, Phillip, no good at all," the fortuneteller muttered to the man who was scratching his head with absolute concentration. "The cards say it, I say it, the ticket sales say it—everyone but the man responsible. The Michael Duffy Circus is at the bottom of the well and no way out. Take a look around. We set up this far from the town because we can't get a first-class permit, so we lose customers. Might as well be carnival people. Can't even afford to repaint our trailers. Look like tramps in our worn-out clothes, we do. But you talk to Mister Duffy and you might as well be a tambourine rattling. Well, not me. I'll not be dragged down to a straw mattress in the poorhouse, not Madame Althea Creel. I've plans, I have, and they're not new ones." She laughed up a series of bubbles. "Want me to tell you what they are, you poor lump of cod?" As Phillip dropped his hand from his hair she burst into a guffaw. "You're safe, but I never took a chance yet trusting a human animal." Suddenly she remembered the stranger. Quick as a snake her round, wigged head swerved to face Tallow. "Be off, you scum!" She raised her arm to strike but the boy moved even more swiftly.

"Tallow!" came a small voice from behind the big tent. "Where are you?"

"That's Billy," said Phillip heavily.

"What's he calling for? The dummy can't hear him. Phillip, you take him back to Billy or we'll have no peace this night. But tomorrow he goes."

For an instant the strong man stared dimly into the stranger's eyes as though searching for something to be feared. Then, very slowly, he smiled, stretched out his hand, and gently took hold of the boy's sleeve and began to lead him away from the lamplight. "He's coming!" he called out to Billy. "With me."

Watching them cross the hard-packed, grassless ground, Billy waited in front of his father's trailer, his white pajamas bleached by the moon to a small ghostliness. "I've fixed him a warm bed underneath with Sir William who's as tame as yesterday's popcorn. But first I have to introduce them to each other." He bent down and tugged at what appeared to be an enormous fur rug but at last a snout and two brown ears emerged sleepily. "Sir William,

here is my new friend, Tallow. You are going to take good care of him." The small boy leaned down and kissed the bridge of the bear's nose.

Tallow knelt on the edge of the bedding Billy had prepared and stroked the back of the bear's head. "He likes you already!" Billy exclaimed. "He's grinning!"

But the stranger's only response was to get to his feet and bow twice, once to Billy and then to Phillip. Then he vanished underneath the coverlets as if glad of a hiding place.

"He's an odd one, little Billy," said Phillip ponderously as he accompanied the child back to his trailer.

"That's why I love him," said the boy.

The man chuckled. "You can't love someone that fast. You don't know him."

"Funny thing is, Phil," said Billy as he went up the three steps of the trailer, "that I do. My mother sent him."

Startled, Phillip stepped backward. "Billy, you're daft. Your mother's been in her grave seven months now."

The boy started to speak again but instead his chest shook with coughing. He opened the trailer door and disappeared, leaving the place where he had stood unshadowed.

2

The next morning the circus awakened at first light to the sound of Jimsey's shrill, tinny laughter. Billy popped from his father's trailer, his shoelaces dangling, hair uncombed, and dashed to where the bear and the stranger seemed to be dancing a lumbering, heavy-footed minuet together.

Billy's breath caught in his throat. For one long flash Tallow had become as wide and furred as Sir William. He seemed to fill the same space. And as his head rocked back and forth, Billy could almost imagine his nose was a snout. Then Tallow broke from the gait of the animal, and threading out an invisible something from his right hand to his left, circled faster and faster around the revolving bear as though he were wrapping him up in—"Confetti!" cried Billy. He clapped his hands in applause and was joined by Phillip just behind him.

The trailer door slammed. It was Michael Duffy. "What the devil's going on here? Sleep is hard enough to come by."

"Oh, Father!" said Billy, hopping with delight. "You should have seen Tallow and Sir William!"

"So I'm seeing them," said Duffy crossly.

"No—I mean before! Tallow, do it again!" Billy sighed. "I forgot. He can't hear." Then his face relighted. He puffed out his cheeks, raised his hands, and pretended to be playing a trumpet. His feet stamped out a martial rhythm.

Tallow's response was immediate. He drew an imaginary sword from his belt, brandished it three times in the air and stomped ahead of the bear. Sir William merely raised himself upright. Tallow's performance did not falter. He marched to a position behind him, enclosed the bear's forelegs with his arms and gently urged him forward into a skating motion. Billy's trumpet played a slow waltz.

"Bravo!" shouted Jimsey as the act ended.

Phillip whistled his approval.

Madame Creel, watching from the doorway of her trailer, was silent.

Billy looked up at his father. There was no change in the long, sour face. "He can stay, can't he?" said the boy. "Can't he?"

Even the bear seemed to sense the moment. He nudged Tallow's leg with his nose caressingly.

"He's got to be able to earn his keep," said Duffy at last, and his tones were doubtful.

"Oh, there're lots of things he can do!" urged Billy. "Take care of the animals, help Jimsey and Phillip put up the tent, do the washing."

"Is that so?" The hoarse voice of Madame Creel tore ruthlessly through the high eagerness of the small boy. "And who's to tell him how to do all that—a wizard? Should someone open up his head and plant it full of instructions? You're fools, all of you!" The force of her rage shocked them into stillness. It was thunderous with hate, as though the stranger had done her some unforgivable, indelible injury. Instinctively everyone looked at Tallow. His pallor had become chalk white and his cheekbones ridged hollows into his face. His fingers were laced tight together. Only his eyes spoke for him and they were clouded with puzzlement.

"Look at him!" the fortuneteller shrieked on. "He's dumb as a toad, deaf as a stump, and as useful as a legless dog. And you want him to eat what we haven't got, to borrow what little is left of the great and glorious Duffy Circus—" she threw a venomous glance at Michael Duffy "—to hang around and drive me insane with his staring?" Her voice cracked and broke off.

Billy doubled over in an attack of coughing. Phillip quickly picked him up and cradled him. "Now see what you've done!" he boomed out, his eyes slightly frightened at his own boldness.

"What I've done, is it?" She charged toward Tallow, her huge haunches flapping against each other and aimed a blow at his head. The boy sidestepped as lightly as a leaf. She collided with the bear. A rumbling growl vibrated through the confusion. Tallow leaped in front of the animal and circled his neck with his arms like a halter. The bear stopped and then began to lick the boy's face.

"See what I mean?" Madame Creel heaved out, her breath short. "He's an animal just like that wretched beggar of a bear!"

Billy released himself from Phillip's comforting. "No! No!" he gasped. "You don't understand, any of you! He can hear! Tallow can hear! When Sir William growled he heard it!"

"He's right," said Michael Duffy, stepping forward. "And if he can hear he can learn. Maybe. Let me try." He spoke directly to Tallow. "Sit down on that bench."

Tallow's head tilted as if questioning, but he did not move.

The circus owner rubbed his chin thoughtfully. "I think he may be a foreigner," he mused as if to himself.

"From the kingdom of Hell," spluttered Madame Creel.

"Quiet, woman," was Duffy's comment. "Does anyone here know a language other than English?" he asked. Jimsey and Phillip shook their heads. Madame Creel spat.

"Let me try, Father," said Billy, stifling a rising choke in his chest.

"Go ahead."

The boy pulled a stub of chalk from his pocket and on the trestle-top lined a crude drawing of a house with a road leading from it. He then made a large question mark beside it.

Tallow smiled his comprehension. Then, walking off five yards so that the grove of birch trees bordering the clearing formed a kind of backdrop, he drew himself up into tallness and became someone else.

By gesture and movement the person came clear: alive with a kind of alien grace, slightly lame, almost to old age, but buoyant as though he welcomed the world and everything in it. He seemed to be instructing someone to his left and then with a shift so sudden it was hardly remarked by the onlookers the mute boy, now himself, responded to the gentle commands and was the pupil. Three times Tallow effected the transference, and with such variety it was almost impossible not to believe there were two people on the grassy stage. Then the old aristocrat made his exit into the columned curtain of birches and Tallow emerged alone.

Billy burst into spontaneous clapping. Jimsey was about to join in when the fortuneteller split the enchantment. "What foolery! You'd think the lot of you were babies brought to your first puppet show!"

"Enough," said Michael Duffy, silencing her with a jerk of his hand. "I wish to question the boy." He walked nearer to Tallow. "I now know this about you."

The boy made shutters of his hands and enclosed his ears.

"You mean that though you are not deaf you cannot understand me." Duffy directed his next words to the small

group behind him. "He undoubtedly comes from a foreign country. He was taught by a gentleman of the theater, an old man who most probably is now dead or the boy wouldn't be a stray on the roads. Do you agree?"

Surprised to be consulted, Jimsey and Phillip merely nodded. Madame Creel expressed her disgust by tightening her thin mouth to a slit.

Only Billy spoke. "Father, do you remember that man

who used to travel with us who was a trapeze performer? Fanchon, I think his name was."

Madame Creel snorted. "Took himself off the first week we couldn't meet the payroll!"

Duffy's dark eyes nearly smiled. "You believe the boy is French?"

"Yes. Yes, I think maybe he is."

"Wait here, all of you," ordered the circus owner and strode off to his trailer. In two minutes he was back with a tattered book in one hand. The other was searching its pages. Then with an effort of speech quite unlike his usual clipped brusqueness he said slowly, reading from the small dictionary, *"Vous êtes français?"*

With the promptness of a marionette Tallow bent into a deep bow.

Billy danced around his father. "Ask him some more things!"

"I can't, and if he is to be of any use to the circus it is up to him to understand us, not the other way around. Here," he handed Tallow the book. "Learn," he said. "Learn fast."

"Even fast will be too late," muttered the fat woman.

"Voice of doom," said Jimsey under his breath. "Old bag of doom."

By now Tallow had opened the book, his forefinger rapidly tracing down a column of words. His eyes lighted and he signaled courteously for Duffy's attention. He placed the dictionary carefully on the ground and then went into a series of motions so easy to interpret, so sharply etched, that Phillip forgot to light the cigarette he had taken from behind his ear. Tallow swept, he shoveled, he washed in an invisible tub, he hung what must be sheets on a line, he scrubbed, and last, he held out both arms as if offering his services freely with complete willingness.

"All right," said Duffy. "We'll keep him. Billy, you show him around. Start with grooming Jog. God knows he needs it." He included the others. "Get to it, everybody. We've got a matinee in three hours."

Billy took Tallow by the hand and led him into the one-ring tent. "Now this," he said, "is our tent. It's been mended maybe a thousand times, hundreds of them before I was even born. But it holds in a high wind and is my real home. Especially—" he hesitated for an instant, "well, especially since my mother died."

The older boy held up the French dictionary and shook his head regretfully.

Billy laughed. "Oh, I know you can't understand me yet. But you will if I keep talking, and besides I feel happier when I'm saying something. The way some people like to sing, I guess, or play the accordion. Anyway, you listen if you want to and one day we'll be able to converse, as Jimsey would say."

As they walked he pointed toward a side-high flap in the tent at the back. "That's where we wait to come on. It's another section of canvas, sort of like an anteroom. We keep things in it too, costumes and boxes, because it's dry when it rains."

The two of them had half-circled the outer rim of the wooden ring when Tallow broke away, and climbing to the very top of the long slats that formed the bleachers, sat down and gazed below at the curved sections of blocks that formed the ring, once red, now scraped down to an uncertain orange. Ropes hung from the upper structure of the

tent and the center pole, striped like a giant peppermint stick, was festooned with bright, metal swings and a folded ladder dangled among them.

Billy Bill followed the direction of Tallow's looking. "The ladder is Sir William's. He climbs it. Used to be part of a tightrope act. They quit us." Billy sighed. "Like almost everybody."

Tallow turned quickly and even from the distance that separated them seemed somehow to send forth a kind of sympathy to the boy whose smallness was diminished even further by the size of the tent.

Billy received the message silently. Then he waved his right arm high as he had so often seen the ringmaster, his father, and beckoned to Tallow. "Come!" he called.

From bench to bench with the lightness of a cat Tallow leaped downward until he stood in the center of the ring. He bowed in four directions as though the seats had been filled to capacity and he had just completed a wildly applauded feat.

For a moment Billy's face showed surprise. "But you know how to accept an audience! You must have had some kind of training." Then he cuffed his own forehead with the flat of one hand. "But you can't understand me yet!" He took the dictionary from Tallow and searched out a word. Slowly, mispronouncing it, the question mark in his tone, he said, "*Comment*? How?"

Rapidly Tallow recreated the image of the tall Frenchman he had evoked in the clearing.

"I get it," said Billy. "He taught you. But now I'd better introduce you to my horse. Come." He noticed the tiny nod from Tallow that accompanied the repetition of the last word. "You've learned it—your first word!" Billy impulsively hugged his companion. "Maybe later I could grow up to be your brother!" Then he raced out of the rear of the tent, Tallow following.

3

During the next four weeks the circus moved twice. These night journeys down the deserted country roads were witnessed only by an occasional owl or a wakeful lamb, and the moving silhouette of the procession cresting the low rise of the hills was brief in length and awkward in outline as the three trailers rattled tipsily behind the platform truck that bore the tent and the equipment bins. Only the headlights pronged through the blackness, momentarily brushing light upon the weeds and grasses at the road's edge or suddenly showing the escaping form of a rabbit or a nocturnal cat. And once arrived the dawn hours were spent raising the center tentpole, stretching the canvas and staking down the sides, and unpacking, before Jimsey began his job of pasting up and distributing handbills in the town.

The first flare of curiosity quenched, the people of the Duffy Circus half forgot their new member. Except for his daily chores of gathering up papers, popcorn bags, and cigarette butts after each performance, feeding and grooming the horse Jog, and Sir William, the bear, assisting Jimsey and Phillip put up and disassemble the tent, and once a week sweeping and scrubbing out the three trailers, he circulated within the insulation of his silence around the edges of their lives. Each of his free moments belonged to his dictionary, his door to this newness. Only Billy Bill was always aware of his presence and the friendship he gave to Tallow was a kind of adoption.

But at the end of that time came a day of differences. They began in the middle of the afternoon at the hour of four, when Billy usually rested or slept. Ever since his coughing had become severe, a year ago, his mother had instigated this routine. He continued to honor her orders because it somehow kept her close and sometimes he could almost hear her sweet scolding when he cut the hour short. But today his loneliness pricked at him with tiny horns and he couldn't lie still. He got up, put on his shoes, and went looking for Tallow. He would be somewhere in the woods, not too far from their encampment. He knew his friend loved trees. Billy had surprised him once, pretending a stand of pines were people. Tallow was directing them as though they were an orchestra or a troupe of players.

He hadn't far to go. Seated against the trunk of a willow

so ancient its branches formed a feathery, green cave, was
Tallow, studying his dictionary. For a few minutes the
younger boy just watched him. He would glance at a word,
close his eyes, lean his head back as if he were swallowing
it, then find another.

Billy parted the leaves and stepped inside. "You must
know a lot by now," he said slowly. To his delight Tallow

nodded. He had understood. He sat down beside his friend. "Oh, I do wish you could talk!"

Tallow's shrug spoke sadness.

Billy smiled. "That's all right. I chat enough for ten of us. At least that's what my mother always said."

Tallow's forehead crinkled in a frown. He handed Billy the dictionary opened at the *ms*. Billy found the word "mother" and showed it to him. Tallow nodded. Then he turned to the French section and pointed at the word *mort* —"death."

"Yes," said Billy, "she died seven months ago, early in the spring when the violets were on the ground." He no longer seemed aware of his listener but continued as if to himself. "She loved violets. I used to gather them for her birthday because I never had money for a real present. She told me she liked them best of all." His voice lowered. "She did, too. She never told me a lie."

Billy fell silent into his remembering. Tallow tapped him on the arm, pointed into the distance and then back to Billy, tracing the outline of his face without touching him.

"Yes," said the boy, "she looked like me. Only she was beautiful. Not the way Jog is beautiful or a new trumpet, but, well, more like this willow. She sort of shimmered. Her name was Miranda." Billy's mouth curved. "She used to laugh about her name, said it made her sound like a lady from foreign parts. It was more like a fairy tale name to me." Billy's hand suddenly clutched around a tuft of long grass and yanked it up by the roots. "She's buried near here. They's why we'll push on before supper. They'll never stop to visit the grave. I asked to once and my father took up his ringmaster's whip and slashed at a stone as if it were a dragon. I never asked again."

Nothing stirred under the willow tree. Even the leaves, like listeners, were still. Then Billy sighed and everything woke. "Guess we better get back," he said. "Lots to do, though Jimsey and Phillip have the tent down and loaded."

But when they arrived at the clearing it was empty and each trailer shut tight. Billy knocked on his father's door. A deep voice yelled out an answer to the unasked question. "We're staying the night. Our cook, seer, and ticket-taker is unable to travel."

"Oh, Lord, that means trouble," said the small boy. He took Tallow's dictionary from him and soon afterward pointed to the word *ivre*. The definition was "intoxicated." "This happens every so often." He looked suddenly very weary. "Tell you what, Tallow, let's get out of here. I'll take you to the place where nobody wants to go again. But we better make ourselves something to eat. That's how we manage when Madame Creel gets these spells."

Tallow pointed to where the bear, tied to Jimsey's and Phillip's trailer, was snuffling lazily at the caravan's tires.

"Of course, you're right. The animals first. I'll feed Sir William. You, Jog. Agreed?"

Tallow nodded and loped to the rear of the tent. The old circus horse nudged at the boy's shoulder while Tallow stroked his nose. The gray flecks that splattered his al-

most white hide dappled his broad back as though a ghost
sun were shining on him behind a ghost tree. Then,
quickly, Tallow filled his feedbag and attached it to his
halter. Now only the munch of his chewing and the slow,
satisfied swing of his ribboned tail made him seem real.
Tallow leaned gently against his side, one arm flung over
his back as though he were learning something from this
great beast, retired from all the tournaments but this last
one, a failing circus.

"Tallow! Come on! I'm ready!"

Billy was waiting impatiently at the edge of the wood, a
bulging string bag in one hand. "I sliced some bread and
cheese for us. There's a stream near where we're going to

drink from." He turned and walked into the green shadows. Tallow followed a few yards behind.

Ten minutes later they had just come to the far border of the forest when Tallow caught up with the younger boy and tapped him on the back. He gestured with an ushering motion toward a row of large stones that rimmed one bank of a narrow creek. He pretended to spread a coverlet over one that was scooped out like an ancient throne. He bowed and waited for his companion.

Billy laughed delightedly. "Oh, Tallow, you are so much fun to have around!"

Tallow's face took on a mock solemnity. He became a squire to a knight and knelt on one knee before the royal chair. He took the bag from Billy's hand and spread out the six slices of thick bread and three slabs of cheese with such elegance Billy could imagine a feast as regal as pheasant, asparagus, and fresh oranges from Spain. He joined the charade with a condescending wave of permission as he seated himself stiffly on the boulder. His attendant served him with the first course.

Noting that the other did not eat, he spoke. "You may proceed, squire," and Tallow, dropping crosslegged to the ground, bit hungrily into his portion.

The repast over, Billy slid down from his throne and stretched out his legs on the grass. For as long as it took a passing squirrel to leap out of sight Tallow believed that the small boy, his eyes closed, had fallen into a fragile sleep. But as he watched over him he saw the thin, red-cheeked face whiten, his eyelids quiver, and abrupt as a blow, a dry rack of coughing jerked through him.

Tallow ran to the stream, filled his cupped hands, and bent over the choking boy, tipping the water toward his mouth. Billy gulped it down and a few seconds later was able to control his breathing.

"Thank you," he said weakly. "I was trying so hard to forget where I was it gagged me." He smiled at Tallow. "But you can't understand that many words yet. My mother," he continued very slowly, "my mother is buried very near to us." He saw Tallow's nod of comprehension. "I must go there. Will you come with me?"

Tallow stood erect and held out his hands to help Billy to his feet.

For the next half-hour there was no sound between them or around them, only the soft swish of the tall, coarse grass against their legs as they climbed the gradual rise of a hill. No tree, no bird, no road or house relieved the loneliness of the landscape. Only an occasional thicket of gorse bloomed yellow like a raft on a green sea. And when they reached the summit of the hill even the distances were absent, for the first blur of evening had fallen on the land.

Billy slowed and placed a restraining hand on Tallow's sleeve. He stopped before a shallow dip in the grass and stood there so attentively he might have been listening to the inner sound of silence.

Tallow freed himself from the boy's touch and in a rhythm slow as a funeral drum began to circle the crest of ground. He dipped and curved, his arms outflung like wings, as though he were weaving something around the burial space, a wall of air, a dwelling or a tomb.

Billy watched until the ceremony ceased. Then suddenly he dropped into the cover of the grass and hid his head in his arms.

For a long time Tallow simply waited, standing so straight, so still, he seemed rooted. A night wind now blew across the violet sky, ruffling the grass into wide ripples. Only the gorse did not stir with it, the yellow blossoms now blanched in the half-light.

At last the boy got up and started down the hill without glancing at Tallow as he went. He rubbed his cheeks on his sleeve. And it was not until they were once more among the trees of the forest that he spoke. "I will not be found there again," was all he said, his voice almost a man's. Then his tones sweetened. "You'll think me an idiot."

For an instant Tallow read his face, then he reared into the air, his hands hoofs, his head tossing, and galloped through the tree trunks, a dancing horse. Billy laughed and chased after him, twirling an invisible lasso.

Just as they reached the edge of the encampment Tallow dug his hind feet into the turf and stopped. Billy slapped him across the back. "You gave me a good run, Prancer!" he said and with a sigh that smiled added, "I'm fit only for bed. Good night, Tallow. Good night."

Tallow saw him disappear into his father's trailer before he started for his own bed-down next to the bear. But he was just passing the fortuneteller's caravan when a gigantic shape leaned out and grabbed him by the shoulder muscles with hands as strong as snakes. The boy's fingers fisted in pain.

"You get in here!" hissed the fetid breath of the woman. She hauled him upward like a sack and threw him into the trailer, slamming the door behind him. He had fallen over the arm of a chair upholstered in purple satin. He drew away from the stench of it.

Madame Creel had lowered her bulk onto a bench, her haunches concealed by a card table covered with an orange and green scarf fringed in red. "You'll not leave until I permit it," she said and placed a deck of wilted playing cards on the table that already contained a bottle and a cup. She poured the cup half full and drank from it. A few droplets trickled down the fleshy creases at each side of her tiny mouth. "I've been wanting a chance to have you to myself," she said, her words thick as though her tongue had fattened in proportion to the rest of her.

Tallow flattened his body against the far wall of the trailer.

"Think I'm going to beat you, that it?" She belched out a bubble of laughter. "And maybe I will after I amuse myself with these little darlings." She had taken the cards into her fingers and was shuffling them lovingly. "I'd get rid of you quicker than a beating if I could, but Michael says you are company for his joke of a son. Come closer!"

Tallow obeyed only as far as a foot from the table.

"Closer!" With the swiftness of a cat she thrust one arm forward, grasped his shirt, and pulled him so near her sour breath gagged him. She released her hold but before he could retreat the hammer of her hand had caught him square across his jaw. He staggered then fell to his knees.

"That's better! Stay there or I'll bloody you up pretty!"

She now began to place the cards, one by one, on the dirty brilliance of the cloth.

For five minutes she patterned the cards into groups. Then, her eyes unseeing, she began to talk, her stridency replaced by a kind of hum as though she were reading from someone else's dictation.

"He comes from a foreign region, from a village. He has lived in a barn, unwelcome in the house or the heart of the woman who worked him. In the days of his darkness he met a figure of light, a man, an old man who taught him the language of the earth and sky and what lives therein, how to speak with his body."

Here the woman broke out of her semi-trance and swallowed so greedily of the whiskey in the cup she sneezed a spray of it onto the cards. She glanced hazily at the boy who had risen up from his knees and was standing so near his shadow covered half of her bulk. She did not perceive the strain that pulled at his mouth or the involuntary clasping and re-clasping of his hands.

She returned to the revelations of the deck of numbers and nobles almost reluctantly. "The old man died and the wolves descended." She licked her dry lips. "There was a burning, a fire of hate. The people of the village trapped the instructed one and set torches to the walls and the night was filled with flames. They said he died but the lid of death opened up before him."

Madame Creel's fingers were seized with small tremors. She darted a look at the stranger then quickly away as if there was something to be feared from the pale face shaped like a spade and the deep mystery of his eyes. Fixed on the cards she continued, now in a whisper. "He returned from the valley of darkness and walks with the invisible one who was his master. He carries something with him that shines. He—" Suddenly with both hands Tallow smeared the cards together into an unreadable heap. A few fluttered to the floor. And as swiftly he vanished from the trailer.

It took Madame Creel a very long time to reassemble the deck of cards and her fumbling was not entirely drunken.

4

Duffy was just winding up his knife-throwing act with Madame Creel against the board, outlined now in black-handled daggers, her sequined pantaloons drooping unevenly over pointed shoes not her own but left by the girl who once starred the act. Phillip was ready to come on with his mind-reading turn, when Jimsey in the back tent saw Tallow reflected in his make-up mirror. He beckoned to the boy.

At that moment the music from the tent boomed into drums, their beat marred by a flaw in the phonograph record that now substituted for a live band. The clown shook his head that was already wigged by a mop of red yarn. "A wonder we get a show on at all," he commented as he painted a mouth two inches wide around his own. "And one day Mister Duffy is going to forget the girth of his new partner and prong her through the flab." He laughed and the sound was bitter. "Wish you could have seen this show five years ago. Thirty in the company and five stars among them. Oh yes, we had a circus." He looked intently at Tallow who had seated himself on a crate to the left of the clown. "I like you," he said. "Dumb or not, I like you. Maybe because you're stupider than I am. You see, I used to be somebody, too. Oh, not famous—just good enough at my job to be somebody. But I'm like a balloon. The circus starts to fail and I fail with it." He fastened a rubber ball to the end of his nose. "Madame Creel is one of the reasons. She's stuck me up with so many pins I've got no respect left over for myself. She's made me believe I'm not funny anymore. She's evil, that woman, and I knew it a long time past. I told Duffy and I told Miranda but Miranda felt sorry for her." Jimsey shrugged into an oversized coat patched by so many colors it could have been a quilt. "Now she was a dear one."

Tallow had left his crate and was tentatively exploring the layers of costumes in a battered, black trunk behind the clown.

"Don't know why I'm talking to you this way," mused Jimsey as he tucked a rope of bright handkerchiefs into one sleeve. "You can't understand one word in fifty and you may well be daft in the head—far in the day is what my grandmother would have called you—but . . ." his scalloped eyebrows moved upward in exaggerated surprise, "you seem to care." He slapped the tabletop with the flat of

both hands. "Going daft myself! What are you doing, boy?"

Tallow had slipped out of his own pants and raveled sweater and was now clothed in a set of black tights. Jimsey smiled. "Those used to cover a man three times bigger than you," he said, indicating the sleeves that hung down over the boy's hands, concealing them. "Better roll up the leggings around your ankles or you'll trip." Then he laughed. "You want to play clown, is that it?"

The change in Tallow's face was so opposite from its usual graveness that Jimsey impulsively got up from his stool and pushed the boy onto it in his place. "Go ahead, boy, have fun. You could use a little by the look of you," and he walked to the flap in the tent that led into the ring to await his entrance.

Tallow dipped three fingers into the grease paint and rimmed his mouth with white, then applied a round polkadot of black where his nose was, and instead of vermilion streaks down his cheeks like Jimsey, white ones. Last he plastered his dark hair flat to his head.

Phillip ran from the ring to almost no applause at all and the clown tumbled out in a series of handsprings. There was only one piccolo of laughter from a very small child.

Tallow stood poised in complete stillness for three seconds and then sprang into the ring just behind Jimsey. Immediately he fell into the rhythm of Jimsey's cartwheels, always keeping behind him. Then the clown began a clumsy, rolling dance around the outside of the ring, waving to the children as he went. Tallow lumbered a foot behind in perfect duet, seeming to anticipate the tiniest variation of movement. Jimsey's mouth under the heavy paint broke into a true grin. He led his shadow into the

center of the ring, and facing the audience, began by awkward, unexpected gestures to try to outwit his double. For the first eight tries Tallow followed, then Jimsey hissed, "Miss the next one!"

The clown jackknifed upward and Tallow squatted downward. A wave of laughter rolled from the bleachers. "Now run away from me!" instructed the clown as they came together.

Tallow obeyed and the two of them scrambled in a wild chase back and forth, Jimsey never quite able to touch the elusive, erratic figure in front of him. A crescendo of handclapping rippled from one end of the tent to the other as they passed.

Suddenly Jimsey halted and pretended to sob, his shoulders heaving. For one minute Tallow hopped around him, entreating him to stop. Then he flung his arms around the clown's neck, his legs around his waist and rode him pickaback out of the tent.

Whistling and cheering the audience called them back three times. Three local boys, hired to circulate popcorn, forgot to call out their wares and joined the shouts.

Jimsey was very silent as they sat together before the mirror. He offered Tallow a towel and a jar of cold cream, showing him how to remove the black-and-white smears. Finally clean, the tights restored to the costume trunk, Tallow stepped back a few feet from the seated clown and looked at him as though he were listening, though no words came from the performer. Jimsey raised his eyes to

Tallow's image in the mirror. They were very bright as though banked with tears. He blinked rapidly. Then he spoke. "It's been a long time, a very long time."

He had just turned and thrust out his hand to the boy when a roar of a voice sounded from outside the tent. "Jimsey, I want that impromptu actor friend of yours in my trailer the minute the show is over! You get him there if you have to tie him up!" It was Michael Duffy.

Jimsey withdrew his hand. "The man's angry. I'm sorry. Stay here. I'm due on again."

But Tallow did not wait. Instead he went directly to his roll of bedding next to where the bear lay snoozing out the afternoon. From the middle of the shabby collection of two blankets and a comforter he withdrew a narrow box covered by worn red velvet. Hunched over it, using the bear's body as a wall to conceal his actions, he opened the lid and gazed lovingly at the glory within. It was a gold medallion layered with star-points and centering the glow was set a sapphire as deep as a fragment of a starry sky. He touched the stone and with great tenderness turned the medallion over in his palm and for another uncountable time re-read the inscription: *To the honor of Hercule Hilaire, premier mime of France, with his country's gratitude. Farewell performance, Theatre Henri IV.* And had Sir William been human and awake he would have seen first remembering and joy in his friend's eyes and then a fall of sorrow.

Tallow tucked the now re-fastened box under his belt

next to his skin, picked up his dictionary, kissed the bear goodbye, and walked slowly to Michael Duffy's trailer. The door was ajar.

"Could have been quicker," Duffy said, his expression unchanging. He pointed with the end of his boot to a stool across the table from him. "Sit down."

Tallow sat, his back very straight.

"You can understand me?"

The boy nodded.

"Did you ask permission from me to go into the ring with Jimsey?"

Tallow shook his head and half-rose to leave.

"Sit," commanded the circus owner as if talking to a disciplined dog. But there was no cruelty in his tones.

"Who taught you to move? You are no amateur. You have worked." Duffy forgot to pace his words slowly. "You have a gift, a trained gift."

For reply Tallow held out the dictionary. Duffy took it impatiently and threw it on the table. "Now listen," he said. "You have a family? A father and mother?"

The boy signaled "no."

"You had a teacher. Who was he? No—be still. I remember. You showed him to us that first day—a Frenchman, a man of the theater. Is that correct?"

Tallow involuntarily brushed his right hand over the hidden box but the man noticed nothing unusual. "Do you not wish to stay with us?"

The boy got up, bowed, and started for the doorway. His intent to leave was evident.

Duffy intercepted him before he reached the exit. "You do not understand me. I am asking you to work with the circus."

Tallow bowed again and this time his mouth was up-curved and his eyes eager.

"Good," said Duffy shortly. "I can't pay you. I can't pay anybody. But you will eat and sleep and perhaps learn something. That's all that's left for any of us. This circus is bankrupt. I know that." He seemed now to be talking to himself, looking out through the tiny window into the rose and carmine of the descending sun. "But it is where we have always lived, Miranda and me, and when it goes I will go with it."

He returned roughly, angrily, to the present moment. "But what do you care about all that?" He struck himself across the knuckles with his left hand. "I'm a fool. I'm a giant of a fool!"

Tallow was at the threshold, prepared to slip off, when Duffy stopped him. "I can't give you money but there is one thing I can give. I will put your name on the handbill. I will give you a place in the Michael Duffy Circus." Then he laughed harshly. "But what the devil to call you?"

Tallow went directly to the little window that was lightly coated with dust and traced on it seven letters. For an instant the colors of the sunset seemed to illumine each one: AUGUSTE.

"Auguste," the man spelled aloud. "All right. So be it. That is your stage name. Auguste, the Wonder Boy, direct from the Continent. Now go."

The boy ran back to the bear, erased the goodbye kiss and planted another right between his ears.

5

In the next three weeks they played only two towns, lengthening their usual stay in each because the attendance was better than they had hoped and even with the tent only partially full it was cheaper than always being on the move. They even resumed the selling of cotton candy, Madame Creel the dispenser. Tallow and Jimsey continued their shadow act and by the end of the first five days had added another, with Sir William.

At first Duffy was pessimistic, arguing that the advanced age of the bear made him an uncertain performer, but with Jimsey explaining while Tallow demonstrated that all they required of the animal was a slow, wheeling walk on his hind legs, the owner consented to a tryout before an afternoon audience.

Dressed in what had once been the bandmaster's red trousers and coat, decorated with tarnished epaulets and gilded buttons, Tallow was the dancing partner of the bear who wore a round, beflowered hat over his ears and a chain of red glass beads looped around his neck. Jimsey was the dancing master and affected a comical elegance in a white suit so tight he had to walk like a stick. He carried a long, silver wand, and as his pupils careened together in one mistaken awkwardness after the other, tapped them repeatedly on their toes. Jimsey had chosen for music an

old record of Miranda's whose label had long since been obliterated but that sounded like Mozart.

From the very beginning the children were enchanted into a kind of hushed watching and it was not until Sir William, suddenly seized with enthusiasm for his role, rolled over on his back taking Tallow with him that the laughter started. From then to the very last note it was no longer laughter but hilarity and the three of them had to take seven bows before the dwindling applause finally released them.

And that same night Phillip laboriously achieved the new handbills, typed on blue-bordered rolls of yellow paper. Billy came to where Tallow was already stretched out beside the bear for sleep and with a wide flourish presented his friend with the best copy.

THE
MICHAEL DUFFY CIRCUS

Renowned to all the peoples of IRELAND and EUROPE

PROUDLY PRESENTS

Five Acts of FABLED ENTERTAINMENT

Artistes:

MICHAEL DUFFY, himself, rope, knife, and gun practitioner extraordinary

MADAME ALTHEA CREEL, Seer of all past and future: cards, palmistry & the crystal ball

PHILLIP: Mind-reader, juggler supreme, and acrobat

JIMSEY: World-famous clown

BILLY BILL: World's youngest equestrian and his miraculous steed Jog

SIR WILLIAM: Russia's aristocrat of all dancing bears

AUGUSTE: Wonder boy direct from the Continent

As Tallow slowly regarded the words he seemed to Billy to change, to grow taller and stronger, and when he raised his eyes from the print he looked upward and listened as though from somewhere in a faraway place someone was saying something to him, something that gave him honor.

"Oh, Tallow!" Billy burst into this strangeness. "Isn't it wonderful? I mean you really belong to us now. And I like your new name. Did my father make it up? Or is it your true one? You won't mind if I go on calling you Tallow, will you? You see I get fond of things as I first meet them. I mean if you changed the color of your hair from brown to red I would go on loving you brown." He thumped his friend on the back. "But here I am blattering like a magpie again! Good night, *artiste*, good night!" He ran back to his trailer.

Tallow carefully rolled up the handbill, tucked himself under his blankets, and holding it in both hands, warmed himself against it.

The next morning was a gray one. Rain weighted the clouds but did not fall. Chill scuts of wind tweaked the corners of the tent and scattered the straw under Jog's hoofs as the great horse chewed contentedly on the mash Tallow had put out for him. Sir William was curled up, half under Jimsey's make-up table, for his nap. Madame Creel had not appeared for the meager breakfast concocted by Phillip and the curtains at her trailer windows were still closed. Jimsey had gone into the village for provisions and Michael Duffy had just entered the rear of the tent.

"Looking for new material?" he called out to Tallow, who was rummaging deeper into the costume trunk. "That was a very successful act you and Jimsey showed us. Did you like the new program?"

The boy smiled and held out his right hand to the circus owner. Duffy took it and smiled back. Then he thrust his arms into the trunk and drew out two-thirds of its contents. "Let's see what we have here." He dumped the pile onto the ground. A short, thin stick with holes it it fell across Tallow's feet. He picked it up. It seemed to be a musical instrument. He put his mouth to one end and puffed.

"No, no!" said Duffy impatiently. "That's not the way. Here, let me show you." He placed his lips to the top hole, covering the others with the fingers of both hands. "You must blow over the hole." A single note issued from the flute. "There. Take it. It belonged to Miranda, Billy's mother, but don't play it around me. It opens doors I've locked off forever." He was scowling as he spoke and did not wait for Tallow to gesture a thank you. He would have witnessed the boy's joy if he had wished to trail him into the forest, for five minutes later amid the unhearing columns of oak and birch Tallow was able to make the first thready sounds come alive.

Two hours passed and still Tallow practiced. He had achieved an ascending and descending scale. A crow on a branch above him cawed a continual protest, but the new musician continued, unaware. Then as at last he relaxed, his head pleasantly buzzing from so much expense of breath, he remembered the circus. It must be almost time for the matinee!

Mistaking his direction he raced farther into the woods, but he did not recognize his error until, as abrupt as a wall, his feet landed him on the beginning of a vast lawn. The expanse was divided by hedges laid out in angular designs and centered by a wide promenade bordered by statues that led to the towered facade of a mansion as long and high as a castle. Its gray stone was sparked with mullioned windows and the angled roofs were clustered with chimneys.

Momentarily paralyzed by disbelief, Tallow then whirled about-face and ran with total swiftness through the forest and into the encampment. He was met by Duffy.

"By God, here's one of them!" the man shouted. "Where's Billy? I'll not have this kind of carelessness! When it's time to go on, every last one of us is here and ready!"

Tallow's expression was an apology.

"Well, get going! Phillip will have to manage Billy's act or at least part of it. Tell him!"

But there was no need to inform the circus's inept juggler and for all his turtlelike temperament Phillip was nervous. He knew that he could maneuver only the latter half of Billy Bill's routine—that of strapping volunteers from the audience into a belted harness that swung by a cable from the roof of the tent and then assisting them to mount Jog's back. Some were able to stay on their feet for as long as twenty seconds as the patient horse cantered within the rim of the ring, but most of them, to the wild amusement of the spectators, found themselves dangling, legs and arms swimming the air, above the sawdust flooring. Usually Billy's urging persuaded the children to try, but this time, with an irascible Duffy as substitute, only one very rotund man came forward—and before the wire could lift him a foot from the ground, the inadequately fastened belt slipped and dumped him on his back. The man limped from the ring, cursing amid threats to sue the management. Duffy signaled Jimsey to fill in and sent Jog from the ring.

Two hours later as they sat down to eat Madame Creel's rabbit stew they were allied in such tiredness they ate without talk. Only the owner seemed alert and he followed the last bite by throwing down his fork and speaking in a voice as tight and toneless as a shrunken drumhead. "We're going to spend the next hour and a half before the performance in searching for Billy. If we cannot find him then he will be left to come in when he pleases."

"He'll return in his own time," said Madame Creel, disinterestedly picking her front teeth with a straw.

Duffy slammed his fists on the trestle. "His time belongs to me! He's got his job here and he is damned well going to do it, not go wandering off like a moth."

The fortuneteller dared a second comment. "Fey like his mother, that boy. Always told you so."

"Go tell it to the bear! I'm not concerned with opinions, yours or anyone else's. Get off your backsides, all of you, and look!"

But no amount of looking or calling resurrected the missing bareback rider and the show went on without him, Duffy replacing his turn with a sharpshooting act he had not done in many years, his aim no longer completely accurate. He now watched the last stragglers leave the grounds in the same cast of anger as he had watched them enter. Scattered bits of trash added to the look of abandonment.

"Get to your beds," he commanded the troupe. "I don't care when our star of the western world shows up, no one is to continue the search. Understand? No one!" He stomped off to his trailer, certain he would be obeyed.

And so he was by everyone except Tallow.

It was after midnight before the last light, Madame Creel's, went out. With another twenty minutes' delay as a margin of safety, he finally hurried from the lot, keeping to a low crouch until he came within the protection of the trees. Placing his wooden flute to his mouth he played three notes over and over as he walked. Billy would recognize the instrument when he heard it. The forest, roofed by moonlight, seemed friendly to the small music and responded in tiny rustlings and squeaks as though Tallow were stirring up the underground country of tunnel and root and hole. He advanced slowly but without pause, led merely by a hope. On and on until he began to tire. He tucked the flute under his belt and simply walked, his hearing now finely attuned to the natural voices of the woods.

Then, with the same surprise as before, he found himself facing the rise of the great gray mansion. The light of the moon had made a phantom of it and no lights showed in any of the hundred casements to dispell the illusion.

He had just touched the rim of the flute once more with

his lips and was inhaling enough breath for his three-note summons when a small figure careened around one corner of the house running so fast the gait was almost a sprawl of arms and legs. Tallow stepped behind a tree trunk. The

runner swept past him and crashed through the under-brush the way Tallow had come. It was Billy, and clutched to his ribs he held a bulging brown sack.

Like a true shadow that never intrudes by sound or shape Tallow kept with the burdened boy right up to the door of Madame Creel's trailer where he paused to ease his ragged breathing. Quite unaware of his follower Billy tapped three times on the panel and then let himself in. He closed it firmly behind him. Tallow took up his station just to the left where he would not be seen if anyone came out and listened. The walls did no more than muffle the voices and the words were distinct.

"So the spawn of the devil chooses to return!" came the strident tones of the fortuneteller. "A fine ruckus we had here and Duffy so furious he could have shot us all full of holes instead of the target! What in the name of Saint Anthony happened to you? I told you where the box was kept and no trouble about that—the butler's an old cohort of mine. Speak, boy! Speak or I'll clobber you one you won't forget!" Tallow could hear her spit.

"Stop that!" Billy said weakly. "Now you've soiled my shirt."

"Soiled, is it? Your soul is soiled as dirty as pitch! What happened?"

"The butler made me wait. His people brought in seven unexpected guests for a hunting party or something. He locked me up. I couldn't help it."

"Enough blabber. Now hand it over!"

The stretch of silence was brief. Then the explosion. "But this is nothing! A handful of trash! A couple of rings and two necklaces! That's a rich house not a maid's bedroom! I want the truth! I've waited a whole year to pull this off and now you—" Her voice choked and Tallow heard three grunts and then a squeezed cry of pain. The door flew open and Billy fell out in a tangle like the tumbling of a scarecrow. A fat arm pistoned forward, seized the knob, and slammed the trailer shut.

Tallow knelt by the boy and pillowed his head with one arm. "Help me," Billy whispered. "I'm so tired. Help me get up."

Together, Tallow supporting most of his weight, they walked toward Duffy's trailer. "No," said the smaller boy. "I can't face my father tonight. I'll bunk in with Sir William." But when they arrived at Tallow's nest of quilt and blankets he simply spread the covers for his friend and wrapped them well around him. "But this is your bed," Billy protested. Tallow smiled and pointed to the heap of bear just beside him. He plunged one hand into the thick fur. Billy's mouth curved very slightly. "His is a good substitute for a rug," he said.

Then his jaw tensed. "I know," he began, "I know you're not asking me where I've been and what happened but I want to tell you. I have to. Someone's got to know the truth and now while I can still tell it. My father wouldn't understand and maybe not even believe it." A series of dry coughs took his breath, and the paroxysm over, he lay silent for a few moments. A bar of moonlight striped his forehead as though someone had placed a crown of light upon his head. Then he moved and his face fell once more into darkness. He cleared his throat. "I am a thief," he said so distinctly there could be no error in the hearing. "More than once I have stolen for Madame Creel."

Tallow's expression asked "why?"

"When I was eight I took her crystal ball to play with. She said I stole it and that she would tell my mother and it would break her heart. After that she had power over my life. She could keep me or throw me away. I'm like a rabbit who for as long as it is pleasing to her she does not devour. And that's the whole truth."

For one moment Tallow was entirely still. Then, certain of Billy's attention, he rose and stepped out into the full moonlight. He seemed to shorten, to become less narrow, more stocky, younger. He held an invisible baton, waved it once around him, enclosing himself in a circle, a ring, then beckoned something in from the night. He then became the arrival, a proud, high-stepping horse that bowed on one knee to his master. Then together, horse and rider began a prancing figure eight to the tempo of a waltz.

The boy was sitting up now, the blankets fallen from his shoulders.

The phantom pair went into the swing of a canter and now the rider turned like a slow top, his arms outstretched, rising and falling with the gait of the horse. He somersaulted twice above the broad back and with a jackknifed arrest on the steed's hindquarters, leaped to the ground, and head up, accepted the unheard applause.

"Oh, Tallow!" said Billy almost inaudibly. "That was me! What a great performance Jog and I gave!" He rubbed his hands through his tousled hair. "But what am I saying? That wasn't me at all. That was—"

Quick as a bird Tallow put his forefinger to Billy's mouth, blocking the next words. He took off an imaginary cap and made a low reverence to the boy, a courtier to his king.

Billy flopped backward into the softness of the bedding. "Oh, Tallow, is that how I really look? Do I truly?" He sighed as he closed his eyes and in the sound was contentment.

6

The next morning was very different from what Billy had expected. Awakened by the vermilion of the sunrise, Billy had left his chill bed and headed for the trailer when an attack of coughing had staggered him to his knees. Tallow summoned Duffy by pounding on his door and when the man gathered Billy into his arms to carry him in they both saw the flecks of blood that dampened the boy's sweater.

"Oh my God," was all his father said.

So just after daylight he was being tucked into his bunk by his father, the man smoothing the margin of the sheet over and over as if to insure against the earlier misfortune.

Tallow, who had followed them in, tapped the man on the back. Michael Duffy turned his face to him and Tallow stepped backward. The stern mask was gone. The cheeks

were reddened as if by some inner fever. The eyes were blank. But worst of all he had lost control of his mouth. It was jerking back and forth, in and out of an involuntary, meaningless kind of smiling that was so terrible Tallow could not endure seeing it and looked quickly toward Billy.

The boy took a breath to speak then cut it off in order to control the rise of another bout of coughing.

Michael Duffy rubbed the back of his hand hard over his quivering lips until he was able to talk. "Don't tell me where you went, Billy," he was finally able to articulate. "I don't want to know. But why didn't you say you were sick? Your mother used to notice these things about you so I never did. I'll send for a doctor."

Billy pulled his father's head down. "No. I'll be all right," he murmured into the man's right ear. "This has happened before. Don't worry. But could Tallow stay with me, at least until the matinee?"

"You'll not ride this day," said Duffy, his tone firmer. "Nor tomorrow if you're not fit. And of course the boy can stay." He straightened, his relief recasting his features into their habitual mold. "I'll look in on you soon." He left quickly.

As soon as they were alone, Tallow extracted his flute from his belt and blew the first phrase of a little tune that rocked like a toy boat. When it was done Billy clapped. "Makes me think I'm three again, in bed and ready for my mother to wake up and come in and give me three kisses. She always did. Not one or two but three. Two for love, she told me, and the third for glory. Play it once more."

Tallow consented and this time added a variation that seemed to underline the joy of the first theme with a broad blue crayon. That concluded, he replaced the instrument under his belt and nodded toward his friend as if to indicate it was now his turn.

Billy smiled. "I don't really miss your not talking," he said. "When I think back I always seem to remember that we did talk, but I have such a herd of questions you can't answer, elephant-sized ones. Did you know the Duffy Circus used to have three elephants? A family of them. But their trainer died and they were too expensive for us to keep. Got sold to a zoo in Dublin. Miranda, my mother, cried when they left. Said they took the heart from us. But you know something, Tallow? Since you came I don't miss them anymore." The boy chuckled. "Funny idea, isn't it?" His tone sobered. "But speaking of substitutes, you'll have to go on for me this afternoon. I know you haven't had a chance to practice and father won't call a rehearsal just for you, but let me tell you how to hold the reins and you needn't do more than just ride standing three times around before Phillip takes over giving the children from the audience a chance to try. It's the look of the thing that counts. You'll be the flourish. The rest is just routine."

For the next half-hour they held close conference and the last instruction given, Billy relaxed back into his pillows. "Why do you want to learn so much?" he asked meditatively. "To earn more? You'll never make your fortune with us. We're coming to the last road, to the last lifting of the tent. Probably our final season." The boy covered his mouth to enclose the deep cough that shook him. Eased at last, he burrowed his face into the pillow away from Tallow. His body seemed crouched in on itself as if in grief.

Tallow tugged twice at a corner of the pillow but Billy did not respond. Then, solemnly and slowly, he drew the velvet box from under his shirt, lifted the lid, and extracted the gold medallion centered by a sapphire. He held it to the sun from the window and it blazed with equal light. He cupped it in his hand and held it before Billy's hidden face. Billy threw off the pillow and sat up. "Oh, Tallow, whatever have you got? It's—it's a dream thing! Where did you get it?" His cheeks flushed. "You didn't steal it, did you? I hope not. It is too beautiful."

The other boy, in that space of stillness where he always became someone else, changed into an old man, erect but frail.

"I know!" Billy cried. "You are that person you told us about when you first came—the Frenchman my father guessed was in the theater. He gave it to you? It was his?"

Tallow smiled a smile that was not quite his own but that partook of a more experienced sweetness as though momentarily he were inhabited by the giver of the golden star.

Billy's excitement had quieted. "He loved you very much," he said and there was no question in his voice. "I understand. You belonged to each other so he gave you what he had."

Tallow's strange smile shattered into a grin that was entirely his. He sprang into the air and descended into the stance of a court jester. On his haunches he jigged foolishly, bouncing as if on wires, waggling his head. Billy burst into giggles and Tallow fell onto his back and silently laughed with him.

"Tallow, you're my favorite clown after Jimsey! But I almost forgot. If you're going on for me this afternoon you'll need my costume or at least as much of it as you can squeeze into. Look in that closet, toward the front."

Tallow drew out the pair of harlequin breeches and tunic that Billy appeared in each day. He held them against him.

"A bit brief in the legs," said Billy, "but they'll do. At least we're the same size around."

The door opened and Michael Duffy came in carrying a tray. "Lunch," was all he said, putting it down on Billy's lap. He merely nodded at the other boy and went out.

"You'll remember to tell Jog why I'm not there, won't you, Tallow? Oh, but I forgot. I'm sorry. You can't, of course." Something in Tallow's eyes brought him to silence. "Maybe you can," he said slowly. "Maybe you can tell him better than me." He waved goodbye to his friend. "Come back afterwards!" he called as Tallow carefully closed himself outside.

The act went better than it had the day before, with Tallow's introduction giving Phillip confidence to conduct the rides more skillfully, and the show over, after calling on Billy only to find him fast asleep, Tallow retired to his shelter beneath the trailer and began to study his dictionary.

He was well through three pages with twenty new words memorized when he saw a troupe of legs before him. He recognized Duffy's and Madame Creel's but the third pair was uniformed.

"No need to disturb this fellow," the circus owner was saying. "Picked him up on the road. Can't talk for a farthing."

"All the more reason to search him," came the harsh voice of the fortuneteller. "Took him on without a reference to his name. Not that we know even that! Called him after a road, we did."

A stubby red hand groped for Tallow's sleeve. He came

out from under the trailer and stood before the group. "You understand me, boy?" said the officer.

Tallow nodded.

"Speak slowly," said Duffy, "and he seems to comprehend. He's foreign."

"That so?" said the officer and he stared intently at the stranger.

Tallow relaxed his body into absolute ease, his expression respectful.

"Any objection if we look into your things?" asked the officer.

Tallow shook his head but did not free the way. Instead he smiled with such clear innocence the man smiled back. "Seems harmless," he commented and moved off toward the tent. "I want another look in back," he said to Duffy.

The boy stooped, prepared to return to his nest.

"Oh no you don't!" It was Madame Creel. "You come right up out of there. I caught on to your wiles. You follow me!" She stumped off to her trailer, Tallow behind.

She kept her words tight in her ballooned cheeks until she was settled in her chair, her huge thighs overlapping its edges, and the boy before her, the door and window shut against eavesdropping. Then they spilled from her thick lips like a stream of saliva. "I saw you go all baby-faced when the law wanted to search you! You're hiding something as sure as there be rats in a barn! Give it over!" She held out a pudgy hand. Tallow shrugged a refusal. Her whole arm flailed forth and swiped the boy across one side of his head, toppling him onto one knee before he could balance himself. He stayed down and ducked the next blow. Winded, the fat woman heaved back into her chair. "Get up, scum! But stand close or I'll let you have it again and next time you'll see stars—my kind!"

Tallow obeyed, his leg muscles tensed and ready to jump backwards at the first sign of a new attack.

"I've watched you and Billy, chummy as glue. Bet the little bastard gave you part of his haul, poor as it was. Did he now, did he?" Her face came forward, rippling the loops of flesh around her neck. "I'd rid myself of him if he weren't so useful, and he knows it. Frightened as a rabbit in a snare!" Suddenly the pouches around her eyes widened. "What's that in your belt?" The question was a hiss. But before she could touch him Tallow was out of reach. He pulled the flute from his shirt and held it up.

The woman shuddered in a cackle of laughter. Then she wiped the drip from her eyelids. "The devil take me if it isn't Miranda's toy!" she rasped. "Used to drive me flighty, always playing it, and only sad tunes, the same ones over and over like she was telling the notes to something or somebody nobody else could see. Thought it got given away with the rest of her trash when she died. Well, that does it! Have to cool the fires." She extracted a bottle of whiskey from beneath the table and tilted it to her mouth. She swallowed until she needed breath, then lowered it. "A toast!" she caterwauled, her grin revealing a row of tiny, blackened teeth. She drank again. "A toast to a lady so far in the day she never came back." Now Madame Creel was rocking with subterranean glee. "A toast to her riddance—to Lady Miranda!" She spluttered a spray of liquor over her bosom and hacked with laughter.

Tallow drifted cautiously toward the door and opened it just wide enough to slide through. He blanked out the noises behind him and breathed deeply of the fragrant night. The stars seemed to gather closer to acknowledge his coming. He drew out the velvet box and held it to his chest. Gently he lifted the medallion from within and touched it to each side of his face, as lightly as two kisses.

Then with a suddenness that strangled he was seized by his neck and dragged back into the trailer.

"I knew it!" shrieked Madame Creel. "You cursed little liar! Give it here!" She snatched for the treasure but Tallow's hand caged it. With a downward chop of her fist as powerful as the fall of an axe she struck his knuckles. The boy's fingers released the medallion into her grasp. "What a pretty!" she crooned. She bit on a point of the star. "Gold it is and that guarantees the value of the gem! Like to know where you stole it but I warrant you'll never tell, will you, dummy?" Her eyes, set like prunes in the dough of her face, glimmered with triumph. "Worth more than all the junk that Billy brought back from that fancy château!" She hoisted herself to her feet and went to the bureau in one corner. Taking a heavy, scrolled key from her left stocking she drew a strongbox from the clutter, lifted the lid, and thrust the medallion inside. She relocked the box and tucked the key back into its bed of fat. "Now scat!" she commanded Tallow, putting the bottle to her mouth and gurgling down what remained of its contents.

The boy seemed somehow shrunken as he stepped once more into the muted moonlight, and his muscles, once as accurate as a deer's, cramped and caused him to stumble as he ran from the encampment and into the columned birches. He slowed, his eyes unseeing, and collided with the trunk of an aged oak. He flung his arms around the scored bark and pressed his cheek into its welcome roughness. For a long time he simply stayed as he was, then, as though tapped on the shoulder, he half-turned and looked into the grove of trees. He released his hold and began to thread his way back, dreamily, as though led.

7

A week later with a half-hour to go before the evening show only a third of the seats were filled. The calls of the peanut and popcorn vendors were halfhearted, as though what they hoped to sell was not worth eating.

Jimsey and Tallow sat together in the canvas anteroom of the tent before the make-up mirror, changing themselves into clowns.

"Saturday night, too," Jimsey was murmuring. "Market day usually brings a better crowd than this one." He glanced over at the boy who was trying to stroke out the wrinkles in his tights. His young face was old. "What's the matter, chum?" continued the clown. "No life in you lately, like you left yourself behind somewhere. Oh, you do your parts well enough. You always will and that's odd for a person as inexperienced as you, kind of as if you inherited the rules without having to learn them." For an instant Tallow met Jimsey's look, his sadness now advanced into sorrow. "Said the wrong thing, did I? Here, try a streak of blue over your eyebrows." The older man penciled it on for him. "Makes a strange one stranger." He chuckled then resumed his own task. "Let me tell you something, Tallow. Notice you've been hanging around Madame Creel's trailer a lot these past days. Don't know why and I'm not asking, but I'd keep free of her, if I were you. She's a toad who squats all over a man's spirit. Can't explain, not really knowing, but bad things have gone on here. Acts quitting, Miranda dying, attendance so poor you'd imagine we smelled bad from so far off nobody wants to come near. And that toad's right in the middle of it, her and her dirty cards."

His disguise complete, he got up and clapped Tallow on the back. "Heard Mister Duffy say this might be our last town so let's give it the best!"

Tallow's attention surfaced and he impulsively touched the clown's arm as if to comfort. Jimsey laughed. "Oh, I've got a family in the south be glad to have me home. You have anybody?"

Tallow gestured to where a tear in the tent showed stars.

Jimsey paused in thoughtfulness. "Maybe they are your people. The world's awhirl with wonders and just maybe—" He squeezed the rubber ball that blew air into his high hat. It danced on his head. "Let's go!"

But for all Jimsey's desire to achieve a special performance, a kind of jinx showed stronger. Phillip's always uncertain juggling was so ludicrous with one fumble after another that before Jimsey could turn it into a comedy the other man had run from the ring. Even some of the children in the bleachers booed, and when Duffy was halfway through the knife-throwing routine with Madame Creel the enormous target, someone started a tide of laughter that humiliated them both. Even the bear refused to waltz. But the final debacle was the horse stumbling on a stone that had become mixed with the sawdust, laming his leg so obviously Billy Bill was forced to conclude the act even before the amateur rides.

The only successful turn was the two clowns and both Jimsey and Tallow improvised double their usual time until Duffy signaled the finale and at last the misfortunes were over.

The last person gone, Duffy called them together. "I realize that this circus is spooked, that bad spirits have been perching on our tentpoles for a very long time. Don't snigger, Phillip. Whatever you call our damned bad luck, it's true. But tonight was a disgrace. As long as one ticket is sold and one person occupies one place on a bench we promise a show and we give it! Tomorrow there is no matinee, no excuse for fatigue or failure! See to it there is none. Good night."

It seemed to Phillip and Jimsey and Tallow, cleaning out the trash from under the seats, re-raking the sawdust, stowing the props, that all the usual tasks of winding up the day would never end. And when they did each man went silently to bed.

Tallow had just pulled his quilt up under his chin and had relaxed into the rhythm of Sir William's snores, when he heard a muffled confusion of noise coming from Madame Creel's trailer. He got up and looked about him. Every van was darkened. He did not hesitate to stand in the full moonlight beside the fat woman's door and listen.

The voice of the fortuneteller sliced clear. "I say you will! What's got into you all of a lump—a sense of honor? A bit late for that, laddie. Here. Want to sample a glass of the old fiery to give you guts? No? Well then listen to the plan once more." Her tones dropped to a drone that was beyond Tallow's hearing.

The next audible words were Billy's. "I tell you I won't. My mother won't let me."

"Your mother, is it?" An explosion of scorn came from her throat like a giant belch. "She was no better than a ghost when she was alive, wisping around you and Duffy like a herald angel. A rose reared on sugar!"

Now something new to Tallow penetrated the fat woman's voice. Each syllable was skewered, projectiles of steel. Shivers traced down his spine as he listened. "Want the truth? Think you can get it down your craw and keep it down? She knew you were a thief. Yes, she did. Her pretty wee boy just as marked as prison scum. She knew about us—she warned me to stop. Coercing you was her word for it. She even threatened to inform the police. A silly fool she was. I knew she wouldn't do it. She couldn't. They would have taken you from her. Besides I would never have given her a chance."

"So you killed her!" shouted the boy. "You did!"

A brief moment fell between the two unequal fighters and when Madame Creel spoke again the skewers had vanished. "No. No I didn't. This life killed her. The circus killed her. Like you she was tubercular. And now, my little cock, get ready to crow. Move on or else I'll talk to your father. You know the house and how to get in."

The door swung outward and banged against the side of the trailer. A form that could only be Billy's arrowed past Tallow, across the circus grounds and into the forest. Tallow was just about to pursue his flight when a loud thud vibrated the floor of Madame Creel's caravan. He leaped the three steps to the threshold and looked in. The woman was flat on her back, her legs and arms spread wide and from the tiny hole of her mouth issued miniature snores. A last few inches of whiskey leaked from a tumbled bottle across her belly. Tallow tapped the sole of one of her shoes with his toe. Nothing changed. The whalelike lump merely breathed. Swiftly he went to the bureau, found the strongbox that imprisoned the medallion, and holding it securely against his side, once more approached the unconscious woman. He leaned over her and with the same reluctance

as if he were to touch a flame he delicately pinched the top of her dirty stocking between thumb and forefinger to get at the key to the box. But as he lifted the band a roll of fat flopped over his fingers. With a roar and a jerking of arms and legs Madame Creel sat up.

Tallow fled.

8

He paused to conceal the locked box under the fur of the bear. He knew the somnolent Sir William would not stir until morning. Then he raced into the double darkness of the woods.

First he listened, but only the crowns of the tall trees sighing faraway and faint in the upper wind and an infrequent rustle as of some small animal in the brush ruffled the silence of the night. He broke a brittle branch from a pine and walked slowly forward, tapping the treetrunks as he went. Then he remembered the flute. He hesitated a moment before putting it to his lips, his eyes closed as though he were asking something of someone. He started forward and the little tune of four notes that he sent like a messenger into the obscurity seemed almost to sing the lost boy's name. "Billy, Billy, come to me."

A few birds woke from their sleep as Tallow walked the woods, sending his summons before him, and marked his going with single cheeps as they resettled themselves in their nests. Once a fox crossed his path, ears up, eyes shining. But no human reply met his melody. At last, his legs aching a little, he came to a narrow stream where the grass grew tall as reeds. He sat down upon its softness and this time he lengthened the music into a tune he had once heard in France coming out of a church window. At the end of it, the instrument now mute upon his lap, he was aware of someone listening. Was it the fox returned or a cow called by thirst to the little creek?

"Tallow," came a thready whisper, "it's me—Billy. Over here."

Three yards away lay his friend, all but his head made invisible by the high grasses. Tallow stood over him for a moment and looked down at the boy's chalky face. Like a gull wheeling home he spread his arms and kneeling gathered Billy in. Black splotches of blood spotted the boy's shirt and his eyes seemed reset in hollows so deep they were filled with their own night. But his mouth was smiling.

"Play Miranda's song," he said so low Tallow almost did not understand. "But I forgot. You don't know it. Listen—I will whistle it. I haven't breath enough to sing."

A tiny, nearly toneless whistle came from his stained lips but Tallow caught the air. Gently, gently he propped Billy's head and shoulders against his own chest then put the

flute to his mouth and began the first phrase. "Slower, sweeter," said Miranda's son. Sad and simple and brave, the little tune circled the two of them and when it was done Billy's lips formed a single, soundless word, "Again." And as Tallow once more breathed the song into Miranda's flute, Billy's face filled with a light that made it very young and very loved and Tallow knew, even before the frail form slumped finally into the grass, that Miranda had come to welcome Billy home.

For a long time he did not move. He was waiting for strength, not to lift the body of his friend, but to accept his absence. Then, his face stiff with control, he got to his feet, and hoisting Billy onto his back, strode steadily through the endless march of trees back to the circus.

The rest of that night, none sleeping but the animals, and the next morning, was like a continuous play of marionettes. The doctor who signed the death certificate, the coroner who approved it, the undertakers, two men in raven black, Madame Creel, for once silenced though she made a pretense of grief, Phillip, his eyes constantly brimming tears, Jimsey, all his motions slowed and difficult, and Duffy encased in an inarticulate anger, all moved through the hours almost automatically. Only Tallow seemed possessed of himself and at three o'clock on a barren hill where the other graves had either fallen in or vanished, just as the last shovel of earth filled the coffined hole, all of them turned to him as if he would be the one to speak.

Duffy broke the strangeness as he raised his fists to the sky and called out, "Damn all you devils of the world! You took my wife, you took my son, you took my circus! Now take me!"

But no one, no thing answered his cry. Only a brush of wind flicked over the grass and one bird rose from behind a hillock, the beat of his wings loud in the quiet. Duffy stared at each one in turn as if perhaps somewhere here was the reply, but each avoided his eyes. His rage was gone. Defeat had replaced it. "Tonight will be the last perform-

ance of the Michael Duffy Circus," he said and walked away. Still voiceless the others followed, all except Tallow.

He wandered beyond the sight of the upturned ground of the grave as listlessly as the errant touches of wind on the bare hill. But when he came to a mound he halted abruptly and threw himself down into a trench of grass. For a moment he rolled back and forth in it as if to secure for his body a correctly shaped resting place. Then he allowed absolute stillness to take him. And, last, he closed his eyes on the sky.

Once a herd of clouds obscured the sun but Tallow did not respond to the enormous passage of shadow. Later a rabbit in a hurry used his stomach for a bridge over the incline. Tallow's hands did not move to erase the tickling left by the animal's paws. And when the day went into evening, the horizon edged with indigo, the little wind brought a shiver with it and although Tallow's skin began to be glazed by its chill he did not rise. A spider discovered him and spun a first thread across his ankles.

The stars were just showing through the long twilight when below Tallow's ear, from far, far down in the earth, sounds as clear as a song entered his hearing. They were ancient sounds with long-gone voices carrying the tune and their sweetness was as potent as the first rose of the world. Tallow's eyes opened but they looked inward and saw the face of Billy Bill and the music helped him remember the essence of his friend, the gallant gaiety. And before he could wonder about the source of this mysterious singing it ceased. The entrance to this other place had slammed shut.

Tallow quickly got to his feet and started back to the circus.

9

That night, at eight o'clock to the second, Michael Duffy stepped forth in his black boots and breeches, his red ringmaster's tailcoat, his golden baton in his right hand, and his voice strident with a mixture of defiance and pride, opened the circus. For the first time in his career he did not estimate the size of the audience. It was nothing to him, this final day, whether there were three hundred or three onlookers. This was the last performance and it was going to shine.

"Ladies and gentlemen, I present to you the famed and fantastic Michael Duffy Circus!"

Phillip, controlling the music, set the recording of trumpet fanfares on the turntable backstage and suddenly the half-filled tent was golden with triumphant sound. On cue, he diminished the volume.

"We welcome you and with high honor begin the evening with Michael, the knife and whip artist, Master of the Diabolic."

Duffy trotted from the ring and in one minute had returned, his jacket now a short, silver cloak, a cluster of knives in one hand, a ten-foot whip in the other. As he raised both in the air to greet the flutter of clapping, Madame Creel, clothed in a purple and red tunic and baggy pantaloons, a tiara encircling her greasy hair, walked out, followed by Jimsey carrying a large, multicolored flat. Madame Creel took her stance in front of it and with a flourish Duffy cast the first of the fifteen knives. The music

was now a sinister chorus of cellos. The blades flew so fast
and so close to the limp flesh of the fat woman that even
Jimsey, now in the wings, gasped with the audience.

Then, at a signal from the ringmaster, Madame Creel
placed a cigarette in her tiny mouth and Duffy's whip
cracked three times. The cigarette was a stub. From the
folds of her tunic she extracted a long cigar. Duffy cracked
the sides of the wooden ring three times then lanced the
leather snake at her face. The cigar fell into pieces. The
people on the benches cheered and Madame Creel waddled
off while Duffy took his bows.

Restored to his tailcoat and tophat, he continued. "And
now, direct from the Continent, Auguste and his Dancing
Bear, a beast descended from the Imperial Bears of
Russia!"

Tallow swung out in wide circles like a harlequined
top. Then, slowing to the tempo of the Viennese waltz now
coming from the loudspeaker, led out Sir William. The two
of them joined in a dance, Tallow doubling the beat of his
steps to the amble of the bear. Then, so gradually it was
two minutes before the audience realized what was hap-
pening, Tallow seemed to hump himself into a twin of
Sir William, their shape and gait alike. The people laughed.
Now the real bear was the leader and the boy bear fell
out of step, then in again, as if taking a lesson from his
furry instructor.

The record changed to a delicate gavotte and the con-
trast of what they were hearing and seeing increased the

laughing. Just as the music finished Tallow took a paper rose from his belt, and bowing to the ground, presented it to Sir William.

Applause like heavy rain crowded the tent. Both animal and boy bent to acknowledge it and loped together from the ring.

The next act was Phillip, the Mind Reader from the Orient, and for once the liaison between him and Jimsey, who mingled with the audience and repeated their questions with coded indications as to the proper answers, was perfect. The clown barely had time to put on his costume and join Tallow for their comedy of shadows and this too was a hand-clapping success.

Phillip's juggling was next and though not a polished show of skill, served to form an interval before the great surprise of the next act.

Even Jimsey could not believe his ears as he heard Duffy announce it. "And now, dear friends, by very special arrangement with connection and contrivance, we present a figure from the mysterious world of magic, a man who has not consented to appear on any stage, in any ring, for many days and nights—The Great Gillespie, Magician Extraordinary!"

Jimsey dug his elbow into Tallow's ribs. "My God, it's Duffy himself! He swore never to appear again as Gillespie after Miranda died. It was their act, a kind of love story between them. I can't believe it!"

But believe it he had to, for Duffy, who had substituted

his red coat for one of star-spangled blue, was at that moment standing in a single spotlight, directed by Phillip, tossing scarves of all shades from his sleeves into the air in a long streamer.

Madame Creel, propped against the left wing of the performer's entrance, hissed her astonishment. "It can't be! He buried that act as surely as he buried his wife!"

But as the tall man tapped on the side of his hat, lifted it, and drew forth a rabbit to the noisy delight of the on-lookers, Jimsey's face flew into complete smiling. "He's doing it for Billy!" he whispered to Tallow. "It was Billy's favorite thing in all the world!" And as they next witnessed a flight of playing cards from one hand to the other, from the magician's pockets, from his cuffs, even from behind his ears, Jimsey gripped Tallow's arm so hard the boy winced. "By damn and by darling!" exclaimed the clown. "If he can do it for Billy so can I! Quick, Tallow, come with me! I need you!"

During the last ten minutes of Duffy's turn that termi-nated in a whirl of confetti pouring from all his pockets, the clown and his assistant were frantically busy, Jimsey giving instructions and repeating each one three times to be sure Tallow had understood.

But in spite of this rush and hurry, just as the Great Gillespie took his last bow, Jimsey appeared in the ring dragging a large, black trunk. For an instant Duffy looked startled but immediately went into his spiel.

"Now that act so justly renowned in the great halls of English pantomime that has roasted the risibles of Kings and Queens, Jimsey Nimble and his partner, Auguste, in— What Lurks in My Trunk!"

Jimsey bowed then scratched his head hugely as though perplexed. A little run of flute notes muffled out of the trunk behind him. Jimsey shrugged his surprise at the au-dience, then lifted the lid and drew out a clarinet. He shook it as one might a disobedient child, then put it to his lips. It spoke a whine of apology. Jimsey pointed to the clarinet, shook his head, and replaced it in the trunk. He had just begun a skipping little dance when once more the shrill demand of the flute notes. Now somewhat irritated the clown thrust his arm into the trunk and this time lifted out a trumpet. He silently scolded the battered horn and slapped it chidingly. As with the clarinet he allowed it to speak. Its sour tones blatted back at him. By now the audience was united in laughter. Jimsey tossed the instrument back and seated himself heavily on the trunk's lid. He had only begun to smile smugly at his victory over the annoyance when the staccato insistence of the flute sounded again.

Jimsey went into a war dance of frustrated rage. He flung back the lid and pulled forth a very old tuba. Wrapping both arms around it he began to wrestle his clumsy opponent. The tuba appeared to throw him onto the sawdust. His limbs flopping like a stranded fish, Jimsey managed to free himself and the two of them staggered back and forth together halfway around the ring. Then the tuba spoke in such blasts of off-key indignation that applause accompanied the laughs. With a mighty heave the clown fought the tuba back into the trunk and slammed down the lid. The image of despair, silently sobbing, his head clutched in his hands, Jimsey appealed to the people. Immersed in his helplessness, his back to the offender, the lid began to open very, very gradually and the flute's song

was small and sly. The onlookers quieted with glee. Out
jumped Auguste, shimmering in silver tights, a white ruff
framing his whitened face so that only his penciled eyes
and painted grin were real. He never stopped playing, and
as Jimsey saw him he grabbed wildly but the flutist was already leaping across the ring.

The children were squealing and calling out "Catch him! Faster! There he goes!"

Twice they ran the outside of the ring, Jimsey stumbling, stubbing his toes, slipping on the sawdust, the flute player now silently taunting him, beckoning his pursuer with the flute, pausing just long enough to be within reach and then darting forward. At the third turn Auguste streaked for the trunk, jackknifed himself into it and pulled down the lid. Jimsey held both arms in the air in the gesture of a champion, extracted a giant key from his pantaloons, and with stealthy joy turned the key in the lock once, twice, three times, four, while the audience cheered. He bowed pridefully, and nonchalance in his every motion, he seized the rope handle at the side of the trunk and pulled it after him to the actor's entrance, and in the middle of his last bow, shrilling in insolence, high and piercing, came the voice of the flute.

A minute later as Jimsey was helping Tallow to assemble his few props for the last act, still programmed as *Billy Bill: World's youngest equestrian and his miraculous steed Jog*, drops of sweat fell from the clown's cheeks and among them a few slow tears. "Thank you, Tallow," he said huskily. "Thank you for him and for me."

Before the boy could acknowledge Jimsey's words, the empty space between the two performers and the back end of the tent was filled by Michael Duffy, Madame Creel, and an Inspector of Police.

"We've trouble," said Duffy wearily. "It isn't enough to

decide to close my circus, to put myself out on the roads alone, too old to start again, but we've got to end ugly." He turned to the Inspector. "You tell it."

"In this county," said the policeman, reading from notes, "a major robbery took place. Someone was glimpsed by one of the servants of the house running from the grounds near midnight. He carried a bag."

"No chance it was someone from the village?" said Duffy bitterly.

"We don't believe so," replied the Inspector, his silence evidence he intended no further explanations.

"Excuse me a moment," Duffy said. "We have a show to finish. Jimsey, will you get Phillip? He can fill in with acrobatics until we sort this out."

Tallow lightly touched the clown's arm. Jimsey understood. "Tallow," he said, "go for Phillip while I finish assembling the rig for Jog's riders and bring the horse with you." A bright flash from his eyes told Tallow to hurry. The boy nodded and ran through the tent flap.

"You fools!" cried Madame Creel. "There's your thief! That dummy and his secret ways—I knew he'd be the death of us!"

"You have proof, madam?" said the Inspector calmly.

"Proof? Who needs it? He showed up one night like a spook just as we were having supper. Came from nowhere."

Out of breath, Phillip reported to Duffy, listened to the owner's brief orders, and entered the ring with a double somersault.

The policeman turned to Duffy. "Is this fact?"

"Yes," answered the ringmaster. "It is true we don't know and will never know where the boy came from or why. But my son—" his voice hardened against breaking "—my son liked him and he has proved useful as a worker besides being a creature of talent whether he can speak or not. He is French and has studied under a master of mime. That is all I know of him."

"Where did you learn his name?"

"We didn't," interjected the fortuneteller, her jowls aquiver. "Named him after a road and if you'll be so kind as to let me tell my side of it I'll do so."

The Inspector nodded his permission.

Madame Creel stepped into the center of the group, shoving Jimsey aside to make room for her enormousness. "I formally accuse the little bastard of the theft," she boomed from the bottom of her stomach. "Search his digs underneath Mister Duffy's trailer—he sleeps with the circus bear—and I'm certain you will find the stolen articles."

Jimsey whistled through his teeth. "Took them from you more likely!" he exclaimed. "Don't believe this woman—she hates the sight of goodness in anything or anybody!" He raised his right arm as if to strike.

"Hold on there!" commanded the policeman. "I'm not here to settle personal differences among you people. My business is to find the culprit, and if possible return the stolen items to their rightful owner. Go fetch the boy and I'll search his belongings."

"I'll say it different and direct this time!" Madame Creel was almost yelling. "I saw him. Wherever you find the jewels, I saw him coming in that night with a bag in his arms."

"You are formally accusing the person called Tallow?" the Inspector said dryly.

"I am!"

"And the poor cod can't defend himself!" muttered Jimsey and was just about to punch somewhere into the flab of his enemy when with a pounding of hooves the great white horse galloped through the tent and into the ring and on his back like a silver prince stood Auguste, Wonder Boy.

The Inspector started forward but Duffy blocked him. "For God's sake, wait! Let the act finish! You'll start a panic!"

The policeman halted He glanced at Duffy. "All right, I'll let you wind it up but I want that rider."

All at once the men and women in the bleachers realized that this event, even though it appeared so, was not part of the program but both wild and real. The broad white horse was cantering as always around the ring, the rocking of his back in time to the music from the loudspeakers. The single spotlight made a silver column of the lithe figure guiding him. But the difference was the box he held high above his head.

A hoarse cry came from the wings. "That's it! That's my box! The devil pinched it from me! That's where he hid the jewels!"

Auguste hurled the box to the ground. It cracked wide open. A spill of gem stones flashed onto the sawdust. Quickly he slid from the horse, picked up a chain from the heap, drew it over his head, and remounted the animal all as fluently as a sweep of wind.

"Halt or I'll shoot!" a man's voice cut across the ring. Screams spiraled from the bleachers. Madame Creel

grabbed the revolver from the policeman, aimed, and before the astounded Inspector could react, fired twice. A
streak of red trickled down from Jog's mane. He reared,
his forelegs up and fighting air.

Tallow reined his head and dug his heels into the horse's
flanks. With a neigh of pain Jog lunged wildly around the
ring.

"I'll get him now!" shrieked Madame Creel, but just as she focused the gun true on Tallow, the Inspector charged her from behind and she fell sprawling into the dirt.

A scrolled key popped out of her stocking into plain view. "That's hers!" Jimsey cried. "The key to the box of jewels! She is the thief!"

Jimsey raced to the exit as the horse and rider were about to charge through. Then for a split second Tallow turned. The medallion around his neck glowed gold and the spotlight caught the center sapphire, lighting it into a sudden star.

Filled with the almost impossible beauty of what he saw, Jimsey called, clear and reaching, "Take the world, Tallow! Take the world!"

And ever afterwards when the clown took a moment for remembering, he was never certain whether or not, riding behind Tallow out into the night, his arms around his friend's waist, he had seen another boy, smiling and bright with glory.

MS READ-a-thon— a simple way to start youngsters reading

Boys and girls between 6 and 14 can join the MS READ-a-thon and help find a cure for Multiple Sclerosis by reading books. And they get two rewards — the enjoyment of reading, and the great feeling that comes from helping others.

Parents and educators: For complete information call your local MS chapter. Or mail the coupon below.

Kids can help, too!